Hello Kitty®'s
Fabulous Fall Adventure

By Kris Hirschmann
Illustrated by Sachiho Hino

SCHOLASTIC INC.
New York   Toronto   London   Auckland   Sydney
Mexico City   New Delhi   Hong Kong   Buenos Aires

Decorate all of the
pictures in this book with
stickers. The page numbers
on the sticker page will
help you figure out which
stickers to use.

ISBN-13: 978-0-545-00348-3
ISBN-10: 0-545-00348-2

12 11 10 9 8 7 6 5 4 3 2   7 8 9 10 11 12/0

Designed by Angela Jun
Printed in the U.S.A.
First printing, October 2007

Contents

Chapter 1
Summer's End

Hello Kitty looked out the window. It was a bright, sunny afternoon—just the kind Hello Kitty loved best.

"Let's put on our swimsuits," Hello Kitty said. "We can go outside and play with the garden hose.

"That's a great idea," Mimmy said. "I'll race you!"

Outside, they turned on the sprinkler and jumped into the spraying water. A moment later, they jumped out again.

"Brrrrr!" said Hello Kitty, shivering. "The water feels so cold. The air isn't very warm, either."

"You're right," said Mimmy. She was shivering, too. "And look! The leaves on our trees are turning yellow."

Just then, Mama came outside. "They are changing color because the seasons are changing," she said.

"You mean . . . summer is over?" asked Hello Kitty.

"That's right," Mama said. "Fall is on its way."

Hello Kitty thought about the summer. There had been beach parties and swimming, cookouts and picnics. It had been so much fun. It just *couldn't* be ending!

"I don't want fall to come!" she cried.

"Don't worry, Hello Kitty," said Mama. "Fall is fun, too. You'll see."

Hello Kitty knew Mama was trying to make her feel better. But she couldn't help feeling sad. *Fall will never be as wonderful as summer,* she thought.

Dear Diary,

Mama says there are lots of fun

things to do in the fall. But she

doesn't understand. I'm so sad

that summer is over!

Chapter 2
New Clothes

The next morning, Hello Kitty woke up bright and early. "I'm going to have all the summer fun I can before fall gets here," she said. She threw back the covers and jumped out of bed.

But Hello Kitty got a shock. Her room was freezing! Hello Kitty yelped as her feet hit the cold floor.

"No shorts or T-shirts today! I need to wear something warm," she said. Hello Kitty looked in her closet. She found an old hoodie and put it on. It was very tight.

When Hello Kitty left her room, she found Mimmy standing in the hallway. Mimmy wore a tight hoodie, too. The sisters giggled when they saw each other. Then they went downstairs.

In the kitchen, Mama was making breakfast. "My goodness! Look at your tummies hanging out! You've grown a lot since last year," Mama exclaimed when she saw Hello Kitty and Mimmy. "Today we can go shopping. I'll buy you some new fall clothes."

"HOORAY!" cried Hello Kitty and Mimmy. Shopping was fun!

After breakfast, Mama took the girls to the store. She let them each pick out new sweaters, pants, and a jacket. She even let them buy warm, fuzzy boots.

During the car ride home, Hello Kitty felt happy and pretty. *I love getting new clothes. I guess that's* one *good thing about fall,* she thought.

Shopping List:

Sweaters
Pants
Jacket
Boots

Dear Diary,

I love buying new clothes! Mama

took Mimmy and me shopping today,

and we got the cutest fall outfits.

Chapter 3
Apple Surprise

Hello Kitty and Mimmy carried armfuls of shopping bags toward the front door, where they found Kathy, Tippy, Fifi, and Lorry waiting for them.

"We're going apple-picking," Fifi said. "Can you come with us?"

"We'd love to!" said Hello Kitty and Mimmy. "Mama, can we go?"

"Of course you can," said Mama. "Put your bags in the house. Then

I'll give you a ride."

Everyone piled into Mama's car. Soon the friends were at the orchard.

"This is so beautiful," Hello Kitty said. There were trees loaded with juicy red apples everywhere. A big sign said:

Pick your own apples!
Please take a basket.

Everyone picked up a basket. Then they headed into the orchard and started to pull apples from the trees. Before long, the friends' baskets were overflowing with fruit.

Hello Kitty chose one perfect apple from her basket. She closed her eyes, held the apple under her nose, and breathed deeply. *Mmmmm!* It was sweet and tart. It smelled like . . . like . . . why, it smelled like fall!

"What are you doing, Hello Kitty?" asked Lorry.

Hello Kitty opened her eyes and

smiled. "I'm thinking about how much *fun* I'm having," she said. "I'm with my best pals on a perfect day. Nothing could be better than that!"

ORCHARD RULES

1. One basket per person.
2. No throwing the apples.
3. Have a good time!

Dear Diary,

Apple-picking is fun!

I collected a whole basket

full of tasty fruit.

Chapter 4
Hayride Time!

Just then, Hello Kitty heard a clopping sound. She turned around and saw a horse pulling a hay-filled wagon.

"Would anyone like to go for a hayride?" asked the driver.

Free Hayrides Today!

"Yes, please!" cried Hello Kitty and her friends.

"Then hop right in," the driver said. "Don't forget your apples!"

Hello Kitty, Mimmy, and the rest of the gang picked up their baskets. They climbed into the wagon and sat down on prickly bales of hay.

"Hold on. Here we go!" called the driver.

The hayride was so much fun! The wagon bounced and swayed as it moved around the orchard. Hello Kitty giggled each time the wagon hit a bump. Whenever she laughed, her breath puffed out in a little cloud.

"It's cold out here," Tippy said. "Let's put our arms around one another."

"That's a great idea!" everyone said. The friends huddled close.

Hello Kitty smiled. "It may be cold, but I'm nice and warm, from my toes to my heart. I wish this ride would last forever!"

Best Ways to Stay Warm:

Wear a jacket.
Take a hot bath.
Drink something warm.
Hug your friends!

Dear Diary,

I went on my very first hayride today!

The horse was so cute. I wanted to

feed him an apple, but the driver said

it might upset his tummy.

Chapter 5
A Delicious Drink

The wagon returned to the front of the orchard all too soon. The friends grabbed their baskets, climbed out of the wagon, and waved to the driver. "Thank you!" they called. Then Mama drove them home.

"What lovely apples," Mama said when she saw the baskets full of fruit. "They give me an idea for a wonderful fall treat."

At home, Mama told Hello Kitty

and Mimmy to go into the kitchen. She helped them put apple cider, spices, and brown sugar into a pot. Then Mama put the pot on the stove. Soon the mixture was steaming.

Mama used a ladle to scoop the liquid into mugs. She handed the mugs to Hello Kitty and Mimmy.

Hello Kitty sipped the spiced cider. It was delicious, like sun-kissed apples, and it made her feel warm all over. "This really *is* a treat," she said. "Thank you, Mama!"

Just then, Hello Kitty felt her eyes starting to droop. Across the table, Mimmy's eyes were drooping, too.

Mama smiled when she saw the sleepy twins. "Put your mugs in the sink before you fall asleep right here in the kitchen. It's bedtime."

As Hello Kitty got ready for bed, she realized something. *I haven't been sad about summer all day,* she thought. *I guess Mama was right. Fall isn't so bad after all!*

Ingredients for Spiced Cider:

Apple cider
Cinnamon
Nutmeg
Brown sugar

Dear Diary,

Hot spiced cider is my new

favorite drink. It's warm and

delicious and apple-rific!

Chapter 6
Fall Chores

Hello Kitty still felt happy when she woke up the next morning. She was ready for more fall fun!

But Hello Kitty was in for a surprise. In the kitchen, she and Mimmy found Papa holding two rakes.

"What are these for?" asked Hello Kitty.

"Fall brings new chores," Papa replied. "The yard is full of leaves.

You and Mimmy need to rake them up."

Hello Kitty and Mimmy looked out the window and groaned. There were leaves everywhere. It was going to take hours to rake them! Still, Hello Kitty knew that chores were important. "We'd better get started," she said to Mimmy.

Before they could start working, Kathy, Fifi, Tippy, and Lorry showed up.

"What are you doing?" they asked.

"We're raking the yard. It's our fall chore," Hello Kitty explained.

"We'll help you!" said their friends. They got more rakes from Hello Kitty's garage.

With so many helpers, the job went quickly. Time flew as the friends chatted and giggled. In no time at all, the leaves had been raked and bagged.

Hello Kitty looked at the stack. "I can't believe we're done already," she said. "Thank you so much for helping, everyone."

"You're welcome," said Kathy. "We didn't mind. Besides, it was fun."

"You're right," said Hello Kitty. "I guess even chores are *fun* when you do them with friends!"

Fall Chores:

1. Rake leaves into a pile.
2. Put leaves into bags.
3. Stack bags by the curb.

Dear Diary,

I didn't want to rake leaves at first.

But then our friends came to help us.

Our chore turned out to be lots of fun!

Chapter 7
A Crafty Activity

Suddenly Hello Kitty realized that someone was missing. "Where's Mimmy?" she asked.

"Over here!" Mimmy replied. She was standing next to a bulging bag of leaves.

"I'm going to use these leaves for a special project. Follow me," said Mimmy.

She carried the leaves into her playroom. She put paper plates, glue, and rubber bands on her craft table. She punched a small hole in the plate and attached a rubber band to the hole. Then she glued pretty leaves around the plate's edge.

"It's a fall wreath," she said proudly.

"Oooooh!" cried everyone. "It's beautiful, Mimmy!"

Everyone wanted to make one. Mimmy passed out supplies. Soon the craft table was covered with wreaths.

"These *are* so beautiful," sighed Hello Kitty. "I love the pretty colors."

"You don't find leaves like this in

the summer," said Mimmy.

"That's true," said Hello Kitty. *You don't find* fun *like this in the summer, either,* she thought. But Hello Kitty didn't say the words out loud. She wasn't ready to give up on summer . . . yet.

To make Mimmy's fun fall wreath, see instructions on page 47.

Dear Diary,

Today Mimmy showed everyone

how to make wreaths with fall

leaves. They're so pretty. I can't

wait to hang mine up.

Chapter 8
The Best Season of All

It was starting to look like summer was gone for good. After everyone went home, the air got colder and colder. It was even cold inside. Hello Kitty and Mimmy put on their thickest sweaters.

"I know how to warm things up," Papa said.

He went outside and got some logs from the woodpile. Then he piled the logs in the fireplace. Soon Hello Kitty, Mimmy, Mama, and Papa were sitting in front of a roaring fire. Hello Kitty felt toasty warm.

I don't know why I feel so good, she thought. *I want summer to come back. I don't like fall!*

But then Hello Kitty started to think about all the fun fall things she had done. She thought about apple-picking and hayrides, fall wreaths and best friends. She thought about cozy evenings by the fireplace.

Suddenly Hello Kitty jumped to her feet.

"Where are you going?" asked Mimmy.

"I have something important to do," Hello Kitty answered.

Hello Kitty got up and ran to the playroom.

She got a marker from her craft table. In big letters, she wrote "Welcome Fall!" in the blank center of her wreath.

Just as Hello Kitty finished, Mama, Papa, and Mimmy appeared in the doorway. "Does this mean you've

changed your mind about fall?" Mama asked.

"Yes," said Hello Kitty with a smile. "At first, I didn't think anything could be as much fun as summer. But I was wrong. I love fall!"

Mimmy gave Hello Kitty a big hug. "I love fall, too . . . and I love YOU!"

Hello Kitty hugged Mimmy back. "Now that summer is gone, we have lots of great new activities to try. Fall is a wonderful time for fun, family, and friends. In fact, it may just be my favorite season of all!"

Dear Mimmy, Fifi, Tippy, Kathy, and Lorry,

We had fun during the summer. But I think the fall is going to be even better. Get ready for LOTS and LOTS of fall fun!

Your friend,
Hello Kitty

Dear Diary,

The seasons may change, but my friendships stay the same—and I'm always happy when I'm with the people I love!

Hello Kitty's Fall Wreaths

You can make fall wreaths, just like the ones Hello Kitty and her friends made!

You need:
- A paper plate
- A pencil
- A medium-size rubber band
- Fall leaves
- Glue
- A marker

What you do:

1. Use a pencil to poke a small hole near the edge of a paper plate.

2. Poke a rubber band through the hole.

3. Push the front loop of the rubber band through the back loop, then pull

to tighten.

4. Glue leaves around the edge of the plate, leaving a blank space in the center. Let the glue dry completely. (It takes about four hours.)

5. Use a marker to write "Welcome Fall!" in the blank space.

6. Use the rubber band loop to hang your wreath anywhere you like.

Chapter 1 — page 4

Chapter 2 — page 8

Chapter 3 — page 14

Chapter 4 — page 20